Why in the World?

What Are Baby Koalas Called?

A Book about Baby Animals

by Kathy Feeney

Consultant:
Dwight Lawson, PhD
Vice President Animal Programs and Science, Zoo Atlanta
Atlanta, Georgia

Capstone press®

Mankato, Minnesota

First Facts is published by Capstone Press,
151 Good Counsel Drive, P.O. Box 669, Mankato, Minnesota 56002.
www.capstonepress.com

Library of Congress Cataloging-in-Publication Data
Feeney, Kathy, 1954–
    What are baby koalas called? : a book about baby animals / by Kathy Feeney.
    p. cm.—(First facts. Why in the world?)
    Summary: "A brief description of baby animals, including what they're called, how
they stay safe, and how they learn"—Provided by publisher.
    Includes bibliographical references and index.
    ISBN-13: 978-0-7368-6755-9 (hardcover)
    ISBN-10: 0-7368-6755-4 (hardcover)
    1. Animals—Infancy—Juvenile literature. I. Title. II. Series.
QL763.F44 2007
591.3'9—dc22   2006025649

Editorial Credits

Megan Schoeneberger, editor; Juliette Peters, set designer; Renée Doyle, book designer;
    Wanda Winch, photo researcher/photo editor

Photo Credits

Corbis/Daniel J. Cox, 16
Digital Vision, 15
Minden Pictures/Frans Lanting, 19; Globio/Katherine Feng, 5, 8; Mitsuaki Iwago, 4
Nature Picture Library/Dave Watts, 20; David Tipling, 14
Peter Arnold/C & M Denis-Huot, 12–13; KLEIN, cover (koalas)
Shutterstock/Jose Manuel Gelpi Diaz, cover (chick); Kevin R. Williams, 10; WizData, Inc., 11;
    Wong Sei Hoo, 8
SuperStock/age fotostock, 7
Tom & Pat Leeson, 21

1 2 3 4 5 6 12 11 10 09 08 07

Table of Contents

What Are Baby Koalas Called? 4

Do Baby Animals Live with Their Mothers? 6

Do Baby Animals Look Like Their Parents? 9

What Do Baby Animals Eat? 10

How Do Baby Animals Stay Safe? 12

How Do Baby Animals Learn? 17

What Happens When Baby Animals Grow Up? 18

Can You Believe It? 20

What Do You Think? 21

Glossary 22

Read More 23

Internet Sites 23

Index 24

What Are Baby Koalas Called?

Most animals have special names when they are babies. All baby koalas are joeys. Baby owls are owlets. Baby skunks are kits. A baby spider is called a spiderling. And a baby **platypus** is a puggle.

Scientific Inquiry

Asking questions and making observations like the ones in this book are how scientists begin their research. They follow a process known as scientific inquiry.

Ask a Question

Would a panda cub survive in your neighborhood?

Investigate

This summer, examine the trees and plants in your neighborhood. Describe them in your notebook. Next, set up a thermometer where you can see it. Record the temperature each day for one month. Finally, read a book about pandas. Find out where they live and what they eat.

Explain

Pandas eat only bamboo. But you couldn't find any in your neighborhood. And your summer weather is too warm for the pandas' thick fur. You decide that a panda cub can't live in your neighborhood. Write this down in your notebook, and remember to keep asking questions.

Do Baby Animals Live with Their Mothers?

Some baby animals, like most snake hatchlings, never see their mothers. Mothers that have lots of babies at once often don't stay to raise them. The babies know how to survive on their own.

Other baby animals stay very close to their mothers. A kangaroo joey grows in its mother's pouch for up to eight months.

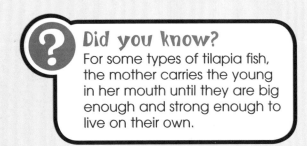

? Did you know?
For some types of tilapia fish, the mother carries the young in her mouth until they are big enough and strong enough to live on their own.

Do Baby Animals Look Like Their Parents?

Zebra foals, snake hatchlings, giraffe calves, and many other baby animals look just like their parents. But not all babies do. When panda cubs are born, they look more like mice. They have pink skin with fine white fur. Black fur begins growing a few weeks later.

What Do Baby Animals Eat?

Piglets, elephant calves, and other baby **mammals** drink their mother's milk. When they are a little older, they begin eating solid food.

Other babies eat solid food as soon as they are born. Rattlesnakes eat mice just like their parents do. Many birds feed worms and insects to their chicks.

How Do Baby Animals Stay Safe?

Baby animals stay safe in many ways. Some have **camouflage** to help them hide. A deer fawn's white spots look like patches of sunlight when seen from above. Cheetah cubs have smoky gray fur that blends in with their grassy homes.

Lots of baby animals count on protection from their parents. A father emperor penguin protects his eggs under feathers that cover his feet. After the eggs hatch, the mother tucks her chicks under her warm feathers.

Some animals find safety in numbers. A group of female elephants called an "auntie **herd**" watches out for a calf. Female lions will fight as a group to save a cub.

How Do Baby Animals Learn?

Monkey see, monkey do. Babies learn by watching adults. A panda cub sees its mother eat bamboo. It learns to eat the same parts she eats.

Baby animals, such as bear cubs and kittens, like to play. But playtime is more than a game. The babies are learning how to sneak up on **prey** and how to fight.

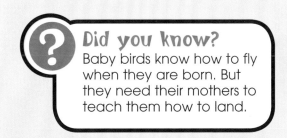

? Did you know?
Baby birds know how to fly when they are born. But they need their mothers to teach them how to land.

What Happens When Baby Animals Grow Up?

Baby animals aren't babies forever. They grow up. Some join herds, **flocks**, or other social groups. Bonobo apes travel with their mothers for about 10 years. After that, females sometimes leave to join other groups.

In time, most grown-up animals find mates. And before long, they have babies of their own.

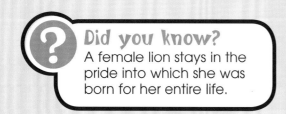

? Did you know?
A female lion stays in the pride into which she was born for her entire life.

A newborn Tasmanian devil joey must race for its life. About 50 other joeys are born at the same time. Inside the mother's pouch, they all fight for one of only four nipples. Only the four joeys that succeed will get the milk they need to live.

You've probably seen human babies suck their thumbs to feel safe. An elephant calf "sucks" its trunk in the same way. Have you ever seen any other baby animals act like a human baby? What did they do?

21

GLOSSARY

camouflage (KAM-uh-flahzh)—coloring or covering that makes animals, people, and objects look like their surroundings

flock (FLOK)—a group of animals of one kind that live, travel, or feed together

herd (HURD)—a large group of animals, as in a herd of cows or elephants

mammal (MAM-uhl)—a warm-blooded animal that has a backbone and feeds milk to its young; mammals also have hair; most mammals give live birth to their young.

platypus (PLAT-uh-puhss)—an Australian mammal with webbed feet and a broad bill; the platypus is one of the few mammals that lay eggs.

prey (PRAY)—an animal that is hunted by another animal for food

READ MORE

Ganeri, Anita. *I Wonder Why Camels Have Humps and Other Questions about Animals.* Boston: Kingfisher, 2003.

Kalman, Bobbie. *Animal Life Cycles: Growing and Changing.* Nature's Changes. New York: Crabtree, 2006.

Posada, Mia. *Guess What Is Growing inside This Egg.* Minneapolis: Millbrook Press, 2007.

INTERNET SITES

FactHound offers a safe, fun way to find Internet sites related to this book. All of the sites on FactHound have been researched by our staff.

Here's how:

1. Visit *www.facthound.com*

2. Choose your grade level.

3. Type in this book ID **0736867554** for age-appropriate sites. You may also browse subjects by clicking on letters, or by clicking on pictures and words.

4. Click on the **Fetch It** button.

FactHound will fetch the best sites for you!

INDEX

bears, 17
birds, 11, 17
bonobo apes, 18

camouflage, 12
cheetahs, 12

deer, 12

elephants, 10, 15, 21

fish, 6
flocks, 18
food, 5, 10–11, 17

giraffes, 9

herds, 15, 18

kangaroos, 6
koalas, 4

learning, 17
lions, 15, 18

mates, 18
milk, 10, 20
mothers, 6, 10, 14, 17, 18, 20

names, 4

owls, 4

pandas, 5, 9, 17
parents, 9, 11, 14
penguins, 14
pigs, 10
platypuses, 4
prey, 17
protection, 12, 14–15

scientific inquiry, 5
skunks, 4
snakes, 6, 9, 11
social groups, 15, 18
spiders, 4

Tasmanian devils, 20

zebras, 9